Noah and the

written by Amy McNeil
illustrated by Cristina Pecherle

Published by Tiny Fairy Press
www.tinyfairypress.com
Copyright © 2013 All rights reserved.

Going to bed was not a trip Noah liked to take.
No matter what his parents said,
He would fight to stay awake.

He'd throw a tantrum.

He'd fake a tummy ache.

He'd pretend to be scared
And full of fright.

He'd do anything
To stay up all night.

And tonight started off like every other.
When bedtime came, Noah fought with his mother.
He slammed the door and threw his pajamas on the floor.

He fought and fought until his mother could take no more.
"Off to bed you go!" she shouted, "on the count of four!"

As she counted down,
Noah knew he was beat.
He put on his pajamas and accepted his defeat.

When his mother came back, she was no longer mad.
She knew Noah hated bedtime,
And for that, she felt bad.

"I brought you someone special to keep in your bed.
I know you're sad, but you won't be lonely," she said.

And before Noah could utter a single peep,
She handed him a dragon, a friend he could keep.
The dragon, named Flame, was colored in orange and green.
It was the nicest dragon that Noah had ever seen.

Noah thanked his Mom and looked the dragon in the eye.
He was suddenly tired, though he didn't know why.
His mother kissed him on the forehead,
Tucked him into bed,
And off to sleep, Noah would soon head.

But before he did, Noah hugged the dragon and said,
"I wish going to bed could be more fun."
Little did he know, his wish would come true,
Before the night was done.

The dragon, you see, had a secret that nobody knew.
When a child fell asleep,
Into the dream, the dragon flew.

Flame was the most special of dragons.
He could fly over trees and castles and wagons.
And that night, as Noah slept with Flame by his side,
Off to Dreamland they would go, on a fantastical ride.

It wasn't long before the two did arrive.
"Open your eyes," said Flame, "on the count of five."

Noah opened his eyes, slowly at first,
And what he saw, made him so happy,
He thought he would burst.

There were children playing everywhere,
And none of them seemed to have a care.

There was a girl on a seesaw with a pig in a wig,
And a funny circus monkey dancing an Irish jig.

There were trees made of lollipops,
A dinosaur that did belly flops,

A big red train that said, "Chu-Chu-Chu,"
And a kangaroo playing a kazoo.

Noah rubbed his eyes again and again.
He finally stopped, though I don't know when.

The amazing sights he saw, he couldn't believe.
"Could it really be real?" he asked, "Or do my eyes deceive?"
"Anything can be real," said Flame, "so long as you believe."

And high in the sky, together they flew,
Looking for adventures and things for Noah to do.

There was a great big castle where Noah could go on a quest,
And search for lots of candies and a great big golden chest.

And up to Mount Chocolate, he could ride a gondola.

Or drink from a volcano filled with Coca-Cola.

He could take a hike in a forest made of candy canes,

Or ride on a horse like a cowboy crossing the plains.

Noah smiled and smiled, as he stood next to Flame.
"I love this place," he said, "I'm so glad I came."

"That's just what I thought you would say," said Flame with a laugh.
"And if there's anything else you want, here comes your staff."

There was a waiter, a maid, and a cook,
And even a librarian reading a book.

There was a musician playing a flute,
And off to the side was a man in a suit.
First he gave a wave and then a salute.

"I am your lawyer," he said with repute.
"I will protect you in any dispute."

The more Noah looked around, the more he liked what he found. He could jump…jump as high as the tree tops.

And when it rained, out of the sky fell gumdrops.

For dinner, he could eat cookies and cupcakes.
And he could play a game for as long as it takes.

He could fill his tummy,
With things that were yummy,
And play to his heart's content.

Noah was very happy,
With this dream he'd been sent.

But soon his thoughts were interrupted by a sound.
Noah stopped and looked all around.
It was a cling and a clang and a ding and a dong.

Everybody froze, and Noah wondered what was wrong.
"What's going on?" he asked Flame.
"Why did those children stop our game?"

Flame shook his head and said,
"That's the signal that it's time to go.
We can't stay here forever you know."

"We've had lots of adventures.
It was a wonderful mix.
But now, we must get you home,
Before the clock strikes six."

"But I don't want to go," cried Noah. "I want to stay.
I want to stay and play here every single day."

"Indeed," said the lawyer with a nod, "This land has a lot.
And to come here, most children would give all they've got."

"But little boys and little girls can't stay here.
Parents don't let their children just disappear."

"You must go home, wake up, play all day,
And do what your parents say."

Noah sighed and wiped away a tear.
"If I wake up, this place will be gone I fear.
How can I be sure that it will still be here?"

Flame smiled and swung his arm in the air.
"Don't worry, Dreamland will always be there."

"Each and every night, when you fall asleep,
Into your dream, I will happily creep."

"We will return to this grand and magical land,
And have as much fun as we can stand."

And so now, Noah goes to bed with Flame every night,
And to his parents' delight, he goes without a fight.

He smiles and smiles as he hugs his dragon tight,
Waiting for the magic of his Dreamland flight.

Note from the Author

This book was kindly written to bring joy to your children. It is very important for me to receive your feedback. Please help me reach a larger audience by writing a short review on Amazon.

Thank you,
Amy McNeil

Other Books by Amy McNeil

Jacob the Dragon Catcher

In this charming fairy tale, Jacob stalks the woods with his tranquilizer gun, looking for dragons to sell to the zoo. As the most successful of all the dragon catchers, he becomes rich and famous. Jacob, however, doesn't feel good about what he is doing and realizes that things must change. Written in rhyme, against a backdrop of beautiful watercolor illustrations, this book tells the heartwarming story of a young man who lets his conscience guide him to a kinder, gentler way of being.

Coco Saves Monstertown

Coco doesn't fit in at his new school because he isn't scary, and the other monsters tease him. When the annual Halloween festival hosts the Scariest Monster Contest, Coco's classmates can't wait to sign up. On the day of the festival, Coco hides out…and strikes up a surprising new friendship. When disaster strikes the festival, Coco and his new friend act quickly to get the situation under control, and everyone learns a valuable lesson. Through a series of colorful, character-rich illustrations, this whimsical story comes to life in a burst of personality that is sure to leave a smile on your face.

These titles are available on Amazon.com in both print and electronic formats.

Published by Tiny Fairy Press
www.tinyfairypress.com

15 September 2016

Made in the USA
Lexington, KY
15 September 2016